*LIGHTS
ON
WONDER
ROCK

LIGHTS ON WONDER ROCK

David Litchfield

Clarion Books

Houghton Mifflin Harcourt

Boston   New York

When Heather was a little girl,
she snuck away from home
and ran into the woods.

Soon, she arrived at a place called Wonder Rock.

Heather sat in the darkness and shone her
flashlight up into the night sky,
where the stars sparkled with magic.

She was hoping that someone
out there would see her light.

You see, Heather had read all about outer space,
and how sometimes aliens came down to Earth
and took people away in their spaceships.

She wanted more than anything to leave Earth
behind and go to live among the stars.

So she flashed her light off and on.

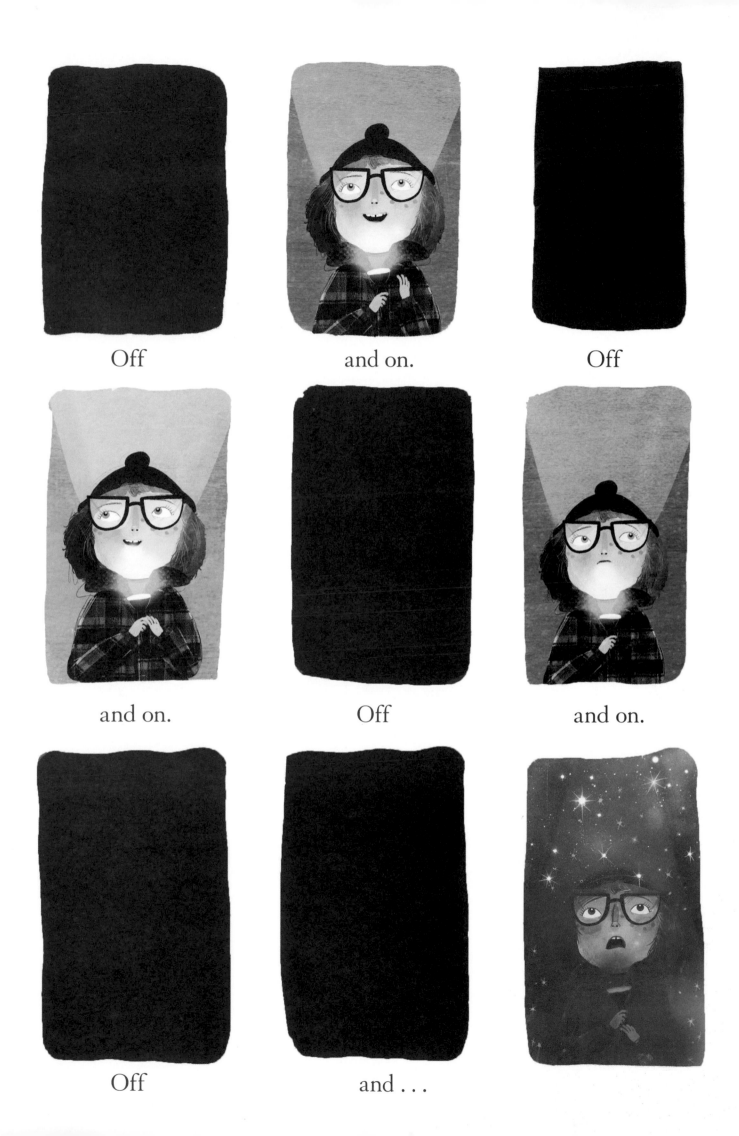

Off   and on.   Off

and on.   Off   and on.

Off   and . . .

Heather was having so much fun with her new friend.

But then she noticed something on one of the computer screens.

It was her family, searching for her in the woods.

Heather ran from the spaceship, shouting,
"See you soon!" to the alien.

Her parents were so relieved to see her that
they forgot to be angry that she had run away.

They didn't even see the spaceship as it silently took off.

Time passed, as time does.

Heather returned to
Wonder Rock again and again.

Anytime she felt sad, angry, or
alone she would sit on the rock,
hoping that her friend would
come back.

Over the years Heather tried
all kinds of new ways to get
the alien's attention.
She tried radio waves,

electricity signals,
lights, sounds . . .
But the spaceship
didn't return.

When Heather was a grownup,
she went back to Wonder Rock.

She needed her alien friend to remind
her that magic was real.

She sat there all night, until the morning
sun began to pour through the trees,
but the spaceship still didn't appear.

Just as she was about to give up,
she heard a voice say . . .

yəwn.

grrrr!

More time passed,
as time does.

Heather went back to Wonder
Rock less and less often.

But every once in a while, she would sit in that same spot and think about her friend.

When Heather was an old lady, she had nearly lost hope,
as people do. But she still liked to sit on Wonder Rock and
shine her flashlight up into the sky. She turned it off and on . . .

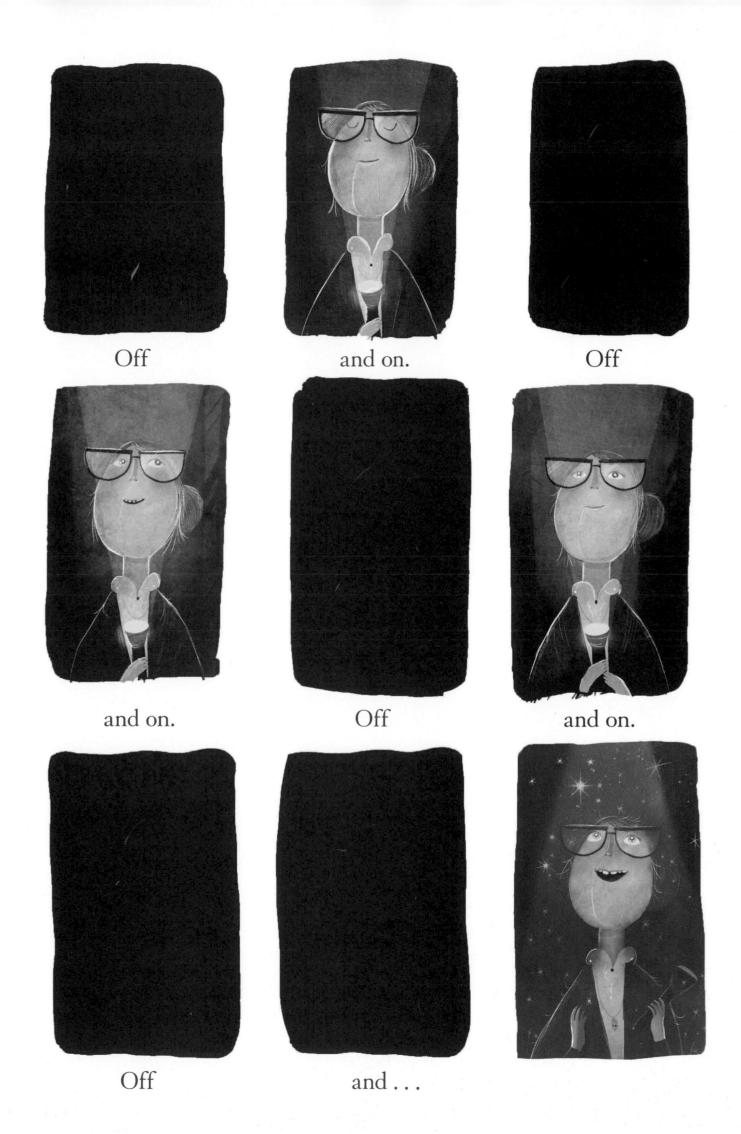

Off

and on.

Off

and on.

Off

and on.

Off

and . . .

Heather's dreams had finally come true.

But as she saw Earth getting farther and farther away,
shimmering blue and green in the darkness,
she suddenly realized what she was leaving behind.

She told her friend that she had to go back, but the alien didn't understand. Wasn't this what Heather had always wanted?

There was only one way Heather could explain.

"My family will be looking for me," she said.
The alien understood immediately.

The spaceship turned around

and went back to Wonder Rock.

Heather was so grateful for
her friend and for the time
they had spent together
among the stars.

But she realized that the magic and wonder
that she had been trying to find . . .

. . . had been on Earth all along.

For Katie, Ben, and George
—D.L.

Clarion Books
3 Park Avenue
New York, New York 10016

Clarion Books is an imprint of Houghton Mifflin Harcourt Publishing Company.

hmhbooks.com

The illustrations in this book were done in mixed media.
The text was set in Granjon LT.

Library of Congress Cataloging-in-Publication Data is available.
ISBN 978-0-358-35953-1

Manufactured in China
EB 10 9 8 7 6 5 4 3 2 1
4500799583